Holly's Christmas Inn…
Where There's Always Room!

A Holiday Story to Warm Your Heart!

Christy Wilburn Nobella Webb

September 2023

A Short Preview...

Holly took a seat close to the back of the sanctuary because she wanted to people watch and one of those people, she intended to watch was Dan Winthrop. Ever since her conversation with Uncle Mel yesterday, she couldn't stop thinking about Dan. Up to that point, she hadn't even considered a romance between them. If the truth were to be told, she had given up on finding love years ago.

Holly checked the time and saw that the service would be starting in about five minutes. She heard a little disturbance at the entrance to the sanctuary and three tornados had just touched down in the form of Tony, Teri, and Tammy. She smiled at their antics and couldn't help wondering where Dan was. About a minute later he came in with Kourtney Petersen at his side, and it was obvious that Kourtney's intent was to keep his undivided attention.

Kourtney looked every bit the model with her tall lean figure, and long beautifully styled blonde hair. She was dressed in a pink suit that hugged her perfect body and even wore pink shoes to match her outfit. Dan was looking around the congregation to see where his three T's had landed, and if it wasn't her imagination, he looked a little embarrassed and frustrated when he noticed she was watching him.

"We're over here Dad," Tammy yelled, and Holly giggled when she saw Dan put his finger to his mouth trying to remind her to talk softly, they were in church after all. He moved quickly to take a seat on the row where his children were, and Holly found it even more interesting when he placed Tammy between himself and Kourtney on the bench. One thing was sure, even if the sermon was boring today, the

3

view a few rows ahead of her certainly wouldn't be! The biggest question now, *why was she feeling so jealous? Afterall, she had told Uncle Mel that she needed to focus on getting the inn ready for its opening, and the last thing she needed to be worried about was dating...and falling in love...didn't she?*

CDW Publishing

Christy Webb has a gift for bringing the fun and magic of falling in love to all of her books. Ever since she was a little girl, teachers have begged her to share her funny life experiences by turning them into delightful and memorable fictional stories. She lives in Utah with her husband and 2 Westies!

Holly recently turned fifty years old and was aware that her community considered her to be an old maid. It was never her intention to be an old maid, she had just never met anyone that she wanted to fall in love with.

When her parents passed away, they left their large cabin to her. For years she has daydreamed about turning the cabin into a warm and cozy Christmas Inn. She has one large obstacle holding her back, and that is her Uncle Mel who lives with her and is unpleasant and has not worked for the last ten years. She gave him an ultimatum to either start helping with the daily chores or he has two weeks to move out.

While shopping at an outlet store to purchase bedding for her inn, three rambunctious children hit her cart with their cart knocking half of her bedding onto the floor! As she begins to pick up her merchandise, an apologetic and very handsome father, Dan Winthrop, introduces himself as a widower of the three tornados that just ran into her cart. Pleasantries are exchanged…and maybe there's hope of changing her status from an old maid to a very happily married woman!

Get a cozy blanket, a hot beverage, and get ready to cuddle up in front of a fireplace with Christy Webb's heartwarming Christmas story!

Dedicated to my husband, Dean Webb, who brings the JOY
to my Christmas holidays!

Happy Holidays to my wonderful readers!

May they be Merry and Bright!

CHAPTER 1

MIDDLE OF OCTOBER

Holly sat down in her rocking chair by the fireplace after she finished straightening and cleaning up the dinner dishes. The nights were growing colder as the fall weather moved closer and closer to the winter months. The fire crackled and popped as the flames hungrily licked at the large dry log Holly had placed on the top of the fire before sitting down.

Holly recently turned fifty years old at the beginning of October, and knew that the community she lived in considered her to be an old maid. It was never her desire to be an old maid, she had just never met anyone that she wanted to fall in love with. She was petite with shoulder length strawberry-blonde hair, a porcelain complexion with freckles, an average nose and a beautiful smile with white teeth. Her metabolism must still be working because she still had a nice figure and on occasion, she was still whistled at by appreciative onlookers.

She lived in a good-sized cabin on the outskirts of Panguitch, Utah with her uncle, Mel, who was not the most pleasant person to live with. Uncle Mel had lost his job and had moved in with her family, promising it would only be for a short time until he got back on his feet. Unfortunately, that was ten years ago, and Holly could tell that he didn't have any plans to move out. He was still unemployed, and now that her parents had passed away, he was hoping to claim the cabin for himself.

Holly was grateful that her parents had left a will and had made it perfectly clear that the cabin had been left solely to her. As she rocked back and forth in her rocking chair, she daydreamed about several plans she had for the cabin. With the Christmas holidays coming up, she had always wanted to dress it up and turn it into a real inn where people could come and stay for the holidays. Her daydreams were abruptly interrupted when Mel bellowed, "I'm still hungry!"

"There's leftover meatloaf in the refrigerator, or you can make yourself a sandwich."

"I want you to make me something."

"Mel, I've been on my feet all day, and I'm tired. I just barely sat down after cleaning up the dinner dishes. If you're hungry, you get up and fix yourself something."

"If your parents were alive, they wouldn't let you talk to me like that."

"If my parents were alive, you might not be living here. I distinctly remember you telling them you were only going to be here a short time…until you got back on your feet. I think it's time you started getting on your feet and helping out around here. I am not your personal slave!"

"You're right, you're my ungrateful niece, who isn't even willing to help her poor uncle in his time of need."

Holly wasn't about to participate in Mel's pity party, and instead, decided to change the subject. "Hey Mel, I'm going to turn my cabin into a Christmas Inn for the holidays. If you plan on living here, I expect you to start carrying your weight by helping with the chores. By the middle of November, I want you to put up Christmas lights on the outside of the cabin, and clean up the grounds so it looks inviting and welcoming. I plan on making several Christmas wreaths that I will need your help to hang so the cabin will look festive for the holidays. We have four extra rooms upstairs that need to be cleaned and ready for our Christmas guests. We'll need a Christmas tree and I'm going to begin my Christmas baking in the next week or so, so I will be ready for our Christmas visitors.

"You can't be serious, Holly! I don't want Christmas guests invading my privacy! Let's just put a stop to all of that nonsense right now! And what about your job?"

"I gave my two weeks-notice today."

"You did what? You've, got to be kidding me, Holly!"

"No, Mel, I'm very serious. I've been thinking about this plan of mine for about five years. I've been saving every extra dollar I could and I'm ready to become my own boss with my own inn. You can either be happy and become a cheerful part of my plan...or I'm giving you your two weeks-notice to move out and be glum and bored somewhere else. What's it going to be?"

"You're not giving me much time. Who's going to hire me...when I haven't worked for the last ten years? You're not being fair Holly."

"I think I've been very fair to you, Mel. For the last ten years, I have been the only one working and supporting you. I'm willing to have you stay here...but only if you can be cheerful and happy...and start helping out. If you're going to be a lazy bump on a log, then I'll say goodbye to you at the end of two weeks. It's your choice."

"I think I've lost my appetite...and I need to go to my room and think about what you've said."

"I think that's a good idea, Mel. I need to know your answer by tomorrow morning...so I can make other plans if you're not going to be here to help carry your load. Goodnight, Uncle Mel."

Holly smiled...as she listened to a lot of muttering from her uncle as he got up and shuffled out of the room. He was in his middle sixties, with a receding hairline, an unshaved face, and a chubby physique from laying around too much. Doing some work around the cabin, would help to put some pep in his step. She didn't want to be mean, but it was time for him to start pulling his weight.

SATURDAY, OCTOBER 15

Holly was up early the following morning making scrambled eggs and bacon. She was surprised when she looked away from the stove and saw her uncle walk in the room completely dressed with his hair combed, his face shaved, and he looked like he was ready to work.

"Good morning, Uncle Mel. You look very nice this morning."

"I hope it's going to be a good morning, Holly. I'm still not happy about what you said last night."

"Take a seat and breakfast will be ready in a few minutes." Holly hoped that her uncle would be cooperative...but time would tell.

"I assure you, Uncle Mel, that I was very serious about everything I said last night. By looking at you this morning, it is apparent that you took me seriously, which

13

makes me very happy. I think with your help, I can turn this cabin into a wonderful Christmas Inn and depending on how we do, we can turn it into an inn that will provide a steady income for the rest of our lives."

"I just hope you know what you're doing, Holly."

"I hope so too. I have worked the last fifteen years at the Panguitch Luxury Inn where I have learned how to clean the guest rooms, and for the last five years I've been working in their kitchen as a cook, and I feel confident that I can cook and prepare some delicious meals for our future guests. Before we discuss anymore about that, I want to know what you've decided. Are you going to work hard each day and support me, or will you be moving out in two weeks?"

"Can I be honest, Holly?"

"Yes, Uncle Mel."

"I don't want to do the work around here, but I also know that I won't get a job anywhere else...so yes, I will cooperate."

"I'm happy to hear that. I also want it understood right now that I'm not going to beg you to do your part every day. If you decide after a week or a month, that you're not going to help, or I see that you're being lazy and not helping, you will have to leave. I have to be able to count on you. Is that understood?"

"Yes, Holly."

"Thank you, Uncle Mel. In order to succeed at this new adventure...I can't be worrying about you not doing your part. I think once we get things setup and going, it will become easier. It will be a matter of maintaining things."

"Are you going to pay me?"

"Your room and board will be your pay. If you work hard and don't complain, at the end of each month, I will provide some type of a bonus for you. You need to understand that it will take time to build up our inn...and we will have to come up with something unique for people to want to stay here rather than the Luxury Inn in town. I can't promise a certain bonus amount each month until we see what kind of business we actually do. You can understand that...right?"

"Yeah, I guess so."

"Right after breakfast, let's go upstairs and look at the four bedrooms. I'm glad we already have beds in each room, but I'll have to buy new bedding and some pretty decorations to provide that cozy look so they'll look inviting too."

Holly was on her way into town to see about purchasing the new bedding. She had been watching the sales for the past few months waiting for the best time to purchase bedding at a good price. Before leaving the cabin, she had put Mel to work on thoroughly cleaning the upstairs bedrooms. She had to admit that she was a little surprised at how cooperative he was being, and hoped he would continue to be so.

She was going to an outlet store where Luxury Inn purchased their bedding. The parking lot was crowded so she knew the sale must be underway. When she walked through the doors, she could see that the store was a huge warehouse where bedding was stacked in rows from floor to ceiling with large shelves holding the merchandise in every imaginable color. If she weren't just starting out, it would have been fun to buy colorful sheets, but for now, she decided to stick to basic white and accent with the bedspread and room decorations.

The upstairs rooms had two queen sized beds per room and she had four twin sized roll-away beds that could be added to a room if needed. It didn't take long to make her selections and she was thrilled when she saw that she would be getting fifty percent off of everything. As she was approaching the cash and wrap area, she heard screaming and laughing, and before she could get out of the way, two children riding on a cart being pushed by an older child crashed into her cart knocking half of her sheets onto the floor.

"Now look what you've done," a frustrated parent said as he raced up to see the damage his kids had caused. He walked over quickly to Holly and said, "Are you okay, Mam? I am so sorry that my children ran into you. Let me help you pick up your merchandise."

Holly was still recovering from the shock of having her cart hit and seeing half of her merchandise on the floor. She was just about to say something, when the store manager came over. "Let me help you with this," he said picking up the sheets. Fortunately everything was packaged in plastic wrap so nothing got dirty or ruined. She began to pick up things as well…and soon noticed, between the store manager, herself, and the parent, it didn't take long to stack everything back on the cart.

"Thank you for your help," Holly said smiling at the store manager and the concerned parent.

"Again, I'm so sorry."

"It's okay…nothing was damaged."

"Are you sure? I'm new in town and was hoping to make a good impression, but it looks like I'll be run out of town if my kids keep this up!"

Holly looked at the handsome man who had broad shoulders, and a full head of brown hair with silver strands weaving themselves between the brown strands on the front sides of his face. As she continued to study him, she saw that he had the palest blue eyes she had ever seen, straight white teeth, and a dimple in his right cheek.

"I'm sure they didn't mean to. Kids get pretty bored when they have to go shopping."

"You are a very understanding woman, who probably has kids and knows what she's talking about."

Holly wished she did have kids, but sadly that blessing hadn't come into her life. "No, I've never been married, but I do like children...and I remember being a child myself."

"I seem to be putting my foot in my mouth no matter what I say or do. My name is Dan Winthrop, and I'm a widower with three rambunctious children, Tony, Teri, and Tammy and we just moved here from Colorado. My kids and I are readjusting to our new life since the passing of their mother and my wife...and thought we'd start over in a smaller town."

"Well, welcome to Panguitch, Utah, Dan. My name is Holly Butterfield, and I'm in the process of opening up my own inn which will hopefully be ready by the first of December. That's why I'm buying all these sheets and blankets and bedspreads."

"That sounds like quite an undertaking! Good luck on your new adventure!"

"I hope once I get everything set up, you and your children will drop by and say hello."

"Are you sure you want my three terrors to come by? You've seen firsthand what they can do!"

"You might have a point there, Dan!" Holly chuckled.

Dan couldn't help admiring Holly...and wondered what her story was. How did this petite, charming woman slip by without anyone marrying her? After getting the wind knocked out of her by his three terrors, she was still pleasant and easy on the eyes! He loved her strawberry-blonde hair and beautiful sapphire eyes. He hoped he might get to know her better.

"It was nice meeting you, Dan. I hope you'll enjoy settling in Panguitch. I'm going to go check out now, before I get hit by another tornado."

"I don't blame you, Holly. Have a good one."

By the time Holly got home, it was lunchtime and she was anxious to see how Mel was doing. When she brought the first load of sheets in, she was surprised to hear the vacuum running upstairs. It looked like Mel was just finishing the second room when she stood in the doorway. When he saw her, he turned off the vacuum.

"I looked in at the first bedroom and I'm happy with what I saw, Uncle Mel. You're doing a great job! How's it going?"

"It's going better than I thought it would. I'm starving, though. What are we going to have for lunch?"

18

"I made some potato salad yesterday, and if you'll get the barbeque going, you can barbeque the hamburgers while I get the tomatoes, onions, and pickles ready."

"That sounds great! Is it okay if I have two hamburgers?"

"Absolutely! You've definitely earned them!"

It was actually a pleasant experience sitting down with her Uncle Mel and eating lunch together. They began sharing ideas for the inn…and Holly could see a happier Mel emerging from inside him.

"I have some more sheets and blankets that need to be brought in and taken upstairs. Would you carry those in for me, while I do the lunch dishes? Once we're finished with that, let's call it a day on the work…sound good?"

"Sounds great to me! I think I'm ready for a nap!"

"I'm excited and very happy with the work you've done today, Uncle Mel. I think we'll be successful and happy if we keep this up!"

"I'm happy too, Holly, and thanks for not just throwing me out."

CHAPTER 2

SUNDAY

Holly left pancakes and sausage in a warm oven for Mel when she left for church. Sunday was their official day off; however, once the inn was up and running, it was agreed that they would both have to do the basics like, cooking, laundry, meal preparation, and room cleaning to keep the inn running smoothly.

It was a beautiful fall morning and Holly looked forward to hearing a Sunday message, and mingling with her friends in the community. She liked to arrive early so she could hear the latest news, and she also wanted to share her news about her upcoming plans to renovate the inn. She would be passing out flyers about her inn, but knew the best way to spread her news in a small community was to tell her friends!

The organ prelude music grew softer when the Bishop stood up to welcome the congregation. Holly saw a quick blur in her peripheral vision and turned in time to see Dan Winthrop and his three tornados entering the sanctuary. She couldn't help smiling when she thought about their stormy encounter the day before! He definitely had his hands full with those three!

When the service was over, Holly walked outside the building and was surprised to see Dan waiting at the bottom of the stairs when she approached.

"Hello, Holly!"

"Hi Dan! How are you and your three tornados this fine Sunday morning?" Holly greeted.

"We're doing great! We saw you when we entered the building and we thought we would wait and say hello."

"That was nice of you! I'd love to get to know the three "T's" better. If I remember right, their names are Tony, Teri, and Tammy…right?"

"Wow…you have a good memory," Tammy said in her tiny voice.

"Tell me your ages, and if you go to school, and what grade you're in?"

Tammy held up five fingers and proudly announced, "I'm five and I get to go to kindergarten! Next year I will get to go to school all day!"

"Congratulations, Tammy!"

"I'm Teri and I'm ten and I'm in the fourth grade."

"Very nice. Do you know how to write in cursive?"

"Yes, we learned that last year in third grade, but I'm still practicing to get good at it."

Holly looked at Tony and waited for him to say something. She wondered if she was going to have to wait all day…because he crossed his arms and seemed determined not to say a word! Dan finally spoke up for him. "As you probably remember, my last tornado's name is Tony. He's fourteen and in eighth grade and he thinks he's the smartest one in the family."

"He's definitely the fastest tornado in the family...I'm not sure yet about the smartest. I won't know until I hear him talk," Holly said with a smile.

"We were wondering if you would like to go to a park and have a picnic with us?" Dan asked.

"That does sound like fun. Would it be okay if I go home and change my clothes first?"

"Yes, we should all do that so we don't mess up our Sunday clothes. We'll be bringing the picnic to help make up for yesterday's calamity. We saw Panguitch park on the main drag as you drive into the city. Would you be able to meet us there in about a half hour?"

"Yes...I would like that!"

Before leaving for the park, Holly talked briefly to Mel and let him know what her plans were. He seemed surprised and wished her a good time. She reminded him of the leftover meatloaf and potato salad, and he was pleased with those lunch choices.

Holly had kept some of her childhood toys and thought it might be fun to bring them along and see if the three tornados had ever seen or played with any of them before. When she arrived at the park, they were there and she noticed Tammy jumping up and down when she saw her.

"I hope you haven't been waiting long," Holly said, giving Tammy a hug when she came up and grabbed her.

"We spread out a blanket for our picnic," Teri said happily. "Follow Tammy and I and we'll show you where to go."

Holly noticed that Tony hung back in the background and that was okay with her. She imagined he was going through his own emotions and needed the space to work through them. Dan was smiling and seemed as excited as his girls to have her there.

The picnic consisted of sandwiches, potato chips, sliced apples, and lemonade. Tammy whispered there would be Twinkies for those that ate their lunch! "In that case, I'm eating every bit of my lunch," Holly said while winking at Tammy. Tammy giggled and Holly enjoyed her enthusiasm.

When lunch was over, Holly went back to her car and brought out the bag she had filled with special things from her childhood.

"What's in the bag, Holly?" Tammy and Teri asked excitedly.

"Something special! These are toys that I played with when I was a little girl...and I thought you might enjoy playing with them."

"Yeah...we'd love to," Teri said happily.

"The first one is a game in a can. We called it pick up sticks." Holly proceeded to open the can and poured out the sticks in a variety of colors on the blanket. "The trick is, you try to pick up as many sticks as you can, one at a time without moving the other sticks. If you move another stick, then your turn is over. Don't get discouraged because it takes practice! Would you like me to go first and show you how it's done?"

"YES!" Teri and Tammy shouted.

Holly noticed that Dan was excited to watch, and even though Tony was in the background, he was curious to see how it was done.

Slowly, Holly carefully worked her way around the sticks picking them up one at a time. When she thought the girls were catching on, she deliberately moved another stick while trying to pick up one. "Oh dear, did anyone see me move that stick?"

"I did!" Tammy cried.

"I was afraid of that! Who wants to try next?"

"I do, I do!" Tammy said jumping up and down.

Holly let Tammy have two turns because it was very hard for a five-year old not to disturb the other sticks. Teri did a little better, and was also given two turns.

"Would you like to try Dan?"

"Come on, daddy, it's hard!"

There were lots of giggles and laughs when Dan got down on the blanket and tried. "Would you like to try Tony?" He shook his head, so Holly took out her frisbee and threw it to him. Even though it surprised him, he was still able to catch it. "Good catch, Tony," Holly complimented him.

He and Dan started their own game of frisbee toss, and Holly got out her jacks and a ball.

All in all, it was a successful picnic, and everyone had a good time, including Tony! "Thank you for inviting me on this picnic. It sure was a lot of fun! We'll have to do it again."

On her drive home, Holly couldn't remember the last time she had that much fun...and wondered if Dan had enjoyed himself. He certainly seemed pleased to see his girls having fun, and even Tony smiled and laughed while tossing the frisbee.

Holly was surprised to see that Mel had cleaned up the kitchen after eating his lunch. She wondered why she hadn't given him his two weeks-notice sooner. She was really beginning to enjoy the new Mel.

She decided to go to bed early that night...and was happy and a little nervous when she realized she only had two more weeks on her job at Luxury Inn...and then she'd be on her own...hopefully for the rest of her working days...if things went as planned!

NOVEMBER

The month of November made its entrance with a brisk cool breeze forcing the trees to surrender their remaining leaves. Holly looked out the front window of the cabin and watched Mel's pile of leaves spin like a miniature tornado when the wind blew by, reminding her of three other tornados she had recently encountered who had caused similar mayhem! Now that her last two weeks of employment with the Luxury Inn were finally behind her, Holly realized that she had been so wrapped up with her responsibilities, she hadn't even had a spare minute to think about Dan or his three T's. Come to think of it, she hadn't seen the little terrors at church for the last two weeks either. She hoped things were okay. She felt a nudging impression that she needed to check on them, but how could she with the opening of her inn fast approaching and no phone number to call them?

She placed the last sheet of chocolate chip cookies in the oven and was planning on mixing up some batter for some oatmeal raisin cookies, but couldn't get the nudging impression out of her mind that she needed to check on Dan and his children. While waiting for the cookies to bake, she went into her office and grabbed her church directory. As she scanned the names, she decided to call Arlene who seemed to know everything about everyone in the church. She heard the timer beeping that the cookies were done and hurried back to the kitchen to pull them out of the oven, placing them on a cooling rack.

She picked up her phone and quickly dialed Arlene's phone number.

"Hello."

"Hi Arlene! This is Holly Butterfield. I'm calling because I have a concern about a new family that recently moved into the area and I realized I hadn't seen them at church for a couple of weeks and I wanted to check to see if you've heard anything about them. Do you have a minute to talk?"

"Sure, Holly. Who are you worried about?"

"It's a widower, Dan Winthrop and his three children."

"Oh yes, I'm glad you called. The Bishop informed me that his boy, Tony, had appendicitis and had to go into the hospital a week ago to have his appendix removed."

"Oh no, I'm sorry to hear that. Can you tell me how things went?"

"Dan told the Bishop that the surgery went well, however, he did have to take a week off from his new job to be with Tony during his surgery and the start of his recuperation. His daughters have been going to school, which is good. Tony is home now, but won't be able to go to school for another week or so, and I've been trying to line up people in the church to help them."

"Do you still need some help, Arlene?"

"As a matter of fact, I need help on Thursday and Friday of this week. Would you be able to help on either of those days, Holly?"

"I would be happy to help on both of those days. Would you be able to give me Dan's phone number so I can call him and get things coordinated?"

"I'd be happy to give you his number, and I'm very appreciative of your help. If you don't reach Dan, or have any other questions, please let me know, Holly…and thanks for calling."

Holly hung up the phone and hoped she'd made the right decision. It was the beginning of the week, Monday…and she still had a few days to get things done before Tony would arrive. She reminded herself that this would be good practice for her since the inn would be open and ready to take in guests in less than thirty days!

Thinking about that, made her heart pound, and she decided to call Dan right away.

"Hello, Dan, this is Holly Butterfield. Do you have a minute to talk?"

"Yes, just a few minutes, Holly."

"I spoke with Arlene from our church and she told me that Tony had to have his appendix taken out. I'm so sorry, and I wanted to offer my help. I told Arlene that Tony could stay at my inn on Thursday and Friday."

"Wow, Holly, that is so generous of you."

"With my inn opening up in less than 30 days, I thought it would be good practice for me. I know you're busy, so when you have a free moment, please call me back and let me know what kind of diet he's on...and what time you'll be bringing him over, etc. If by chance I'm away from my phone, just leave a message and the best time to call you back. How does that sound, Dan?"

"Sounds great, Holly, and thanks."

"Okay, goodbye for now, Dan."

Holly got started on her oatmeal raisin cookies, and as she worked, she was glad she had purchased the new heavy-duty washer and dryer and had them delivered last week. She wasn't planning on washing and making up the beds for a couple of weeks, but with Tony coming, she might as well get started with that chore in order to make sure she didn't have any problems with her new appliances. She decided to make a list of everything she needed to get done for the opening of the inn, and as long as she kept to her schedule, she would be ready for the opening when December arrived.

CHAPTER 3

WEDNESDAY MORNING

Y ou did what?" Uncle Mel hollered!

Uncle Mel's belligerent reply to Holly informing him that Tony would be coming to stay for a couple of days totally caught her off guard. "I don't understand what has you so upset, Uncle Mel. In less than a month, my cabin, this inn will be open for business. We will be welcoming people into our cabin with a smile on our face. Up until this moment, I thought you had a change of heart."

"Up until this moment, I was hoping you were going to come to your senses, Holly. I can see I was wrong about that!"

"I'm sad you feel that way, Uncle Mel. What are we going to do about it?"

"What choice do I have?"

"You have two choices, Uncle Mel. You either give yourself an attitude adjustment right now and perk up and get with the program, or you have a week to move out and find somewhere else to live. I made it perfectly clear several weeks ago, that I would not put up with your headstrong and stubborn attitude. You have been such a joy to be around lately and I was hoping we wouldn't have to revisit this subject. I'm serious, Uncle Mel, what's it going to be?"

"I'll stay...but I don't have to like it!"

"You're right...you don't have to like it...but I'm not going to tolerate your negative attitude and I better not ever see it displayed around any of our guests or me...or you will be packing and leaving that very day! From this day forward, you better be the best Hollywood actor there ever was, capable of winning an Oscar for your acting ability. Is that understood?"

"Yes, Mam."

"Now, Tony is a young man who is fourteen years old. His mother died earlier this year and he just went through a painful surgery of having his appendix removed. His father is a widower with three children and needs our help. I thought having him stay here for a couple of days would be good practice for us, and he needs kindness and understanding, not a grumpy old man with a rotten attitude. Go wash up for breakfast; I'll be ready to serve in five minutes."

When Uncle Mel returned to the dining room, there were warm muffins and a fruit parfait filled with vanilla yogurt and fruit waiting for him, along with a tray of bacon. It smelled heavenly, and as much as Uncle Mel didn't want to be happy about the situation, he knew he would never have it this good anywhere else.

"I'm sorry for the way I behaved, Holly. You've done so much for me and I hope you'll forgive me for acting the way I did. I want to stay...and I have to admit, I get a little scared about having a lot of people around. I guess you could say I'm a confirmed hermit!"

"I can understand your feelings, Uncle Mel. I get scared myself sometimes. I'm tired of working so hard for someone else, and getting paid so little for my talents. With your help, I think we can build a wonderful livelihood for us, and you might find that it's fun…if you'll fight your fear and negative feelings. I think you have a lot to offer people. You're very talented with your woodcarving, and when you want to be, you're a fun person to be around."

"It's nice to hear you say those things, Holly. I haven't done any woodcarving in years. It might be fun to take it up again."

"Tony, the boy we'll be taking in, is very quiet and acts like a hermit…so you two may have a lot in common. There have been so many unexpected changes in his life this year, I'm sure he is experiencing all kinds of feelings; grief, anger, frustration about having to move to a new place, and not understanding why he had to have a painful surgery. Imagine yourself in his place. How would you feel if you knew you weren't welcome in the place you have to come and stay at until you feel better? We can make a difference by just being kind and welcoming."

"Okay, Holly. I see what you're saying, and I'm going to keep working on myself."

"That's all I can ask for, Uncle Mel."

THURSDAY MORNING

Holly checked her watch again and realized that Dan should be arriving with Tony any minute. She decided to put him in the room that had the bear trail rustic quilt. It had a rough and masculine look to it with its appliqued bears and trees with printed bears and paw prints on mini checks that were done in colors of taupe, brown, eggshell, tan, dark cyan, dark teal, wine, and merlot. Added to the sleeping

32

pillows, were three accent pillows, two quilted bear throw pillows and one dark cyan accent pillow.

Holly was coming down the stairs, after checking the room Tony would stay in, when she heard the knocking at the front door. When she opened the door, she welcomed both Dan and Tony. She could tell that Tony was still in pain by his pale countenance and the apprehensive look on his face.

"You have a beautiful cabin, Holly," Dan complimented.

"Thank you. Why don't we get Tony settled in his room? Please follow me up the stairs." She could tell that the task of climbing the stairs was painful for Tony, and wished she had an elevator. She entered the room ahead of them and quickly turned back the covers on the bed. Dan helped Tony gingerly slip into bed and reassured him that he would be back that evening to pick him up.

"Tony, are you hungry?" Holly asked.

Tony shook his head, no.

Holly picked up the remote to the TV and laid it on the bedside table where it would be in easy reach for him. "I put the remote where you can reach it if you decide you'd like to watch TV. The bathroom is out the door and down the hall to your right. I will come up and check on you every hour to hour and a half. Next to the remote is a bell you can ring if you need me to come sooner…okay?"

Tony nodded his head, yes.

"I'm going to leave for work now, Tony. I'll see you tonight, son."

Dan followed Holly out of the room and when they reached the main entry, he said, "Thank you Holly for all you're doing."

"I'm happy to help out. I was going to make some macaroni and cheese for him for lunch. Will he be able to eat that?"

"Yes. He was on liquids for the first week and is now finally getting his appetite back."

"Is there anything he prefers to eat?"

"He loves plain Jell-o or applesauce, and toast."

"Very good. I do have that on hand. I'm sorry you're having these extra challenges. I hope that you can go to work and not worry. I'll do my best to take good care of him."

"I appreciate that, Holly. I guess I better be on my way. I'll see you later tonight."

Holly decided to do more cookie baking so she could be close by if Tony needed her. She made two batches of dough that needed to be refrigerated before she could bake them. She made a double batch each of classic sugar cookie and gingerbread dough. After covering the dough, she placed each large bowl in the refrigerator. She had made some plain lime Jell-o early that morning and decided to check on Tony to see if he would like some.

As she got closer to the room Tony was in, she was happy to hear that he had turned on the TV. "Hi Tony, I'm coming in to check on you. I was wondering if you would like some plain lime Jell-o and a piece of toast?"

"Yes, please."

Holly almost fainted when she actually heard Tony speak to her. "Would you like one piece of toast or two?"

"If it's not too much trouble, I would like two pieces."

"No trouble at all."

When Holly left the room, she actually felt like skipping down the stairs. Tony was beginning to warm up to her and it felt wonderful. As she was fixing a tray and adding the Jell-o and toast, Uncle Mel came into the room.

"Hello, Uncle Mel. I'd like you to come with me. I'm going to take this tray up to Tony, and I'd like to introduce you to him. He is still in a lot of pain, and he may need to go to the bathroom. I think he might feel more comfortable having you walk down the hall with him, rather than me."

"I guess I can do that."

"I would appreciate it. Would you grab a TV tray from the den and then I'll be ready to carry this tray up."

"Tony, I would like you to meet my Uncle Mel. He lives here with me and helps me around the cabin." Tony watched as Mel set up the TV tray. "Uncle Mel is going to walk with you down the hall and show you where the bathroom is while I finish setting up the food tray."

Both Holly and Uncle Mel watched Tony grit his teeth while pulling himself up into a sitting position. He carefully swung his feet over the side of the bed, and Holly was surprised when she heard Uncle Mel say, "Can I help pull you up, partner?"

"I sure would appreciate it. Thank you."

"No problem."

Tony walked gingerly out of the room following Uncle Mel very carefully. Holly couldn't believe how compassionate Mel had just been to Tony and it seemed totally natural, not a bit forced like she had anticipated.

When they got back, she noticed Uncle Mel helping Tony lower himself back to bed in a sitting position. Holly placed the TV tray where he could easily reach it. "I forgot to bring up a water bottle for you, Tony."

"I'll go get it, Holly," Uncle Mel happily volunteered.

Boy...would wonders never cease! "It's about ten in the morning. I was thinking about making some macaroni and cheese for lunch. Does that sound good to you, Tony?"

"Yes, it sounds real, good. I haven't had that in a long time."

"Here's some water for you, Tony. I went ahead and opened the cap. Sometimes those can be hard to twist when you're not feeling too good."

"Thank you, Uncle Mel," Tony said.

Holly looked at Mel...and saw his grin from ear to ear.

The rest of the day went by very smoothly! Tony ate his macaroni and cheese and another bowl of Jell-o, as well as, a dish of applesauce. Holly was very surprised when she heard Uncle Mel ask Tony if he had ever played Chinese checkers.

"It's been a while, but I think if you remind me how, I could play it with you."

If Holly didn't know better, Uncle Mel was enjoying having Tony here more than she could have ever imagined!

Holly called Dan at work to give him a progress report on Tony, and also invited him to bring Teri and Tammy over for dinner.

"Oh, Holly, that's too much work for you," Dan replied.

"I better get used to it with my inn opening in less than thirty days. I thought I would make some baked chicken and rice with a vegetable. I'm sure your girls would love to come over."

"I'm sure they would too. We'd all love to come if you're positive it won't be too much for you."

"I'm positive!"

Dinner was a success that night...and Uncle Mel shared how he had played several games of checkers and Chinese checkers with Tony, and only won one game! Holly had never seen Uncle Mel this happy.

"Sometime I want to play checkers with Uncle Mel," Tammy said excitedly.

"Let's hope she can do it without having to have her appendix out," Dan answered. "I better go upstairs and get Tony and we'll get out of your hair so you can get some things done."

When Dan and Tony came downstairs, if it wasn't her imagination, Tony had a lot more color in his face and he looked like he was feeling a lot better.

"Thanks again, Holly and Uncle Mel, for taking such good care of Tony today. And thanks for dinner; it was wonderful!"

"You're coming back tomorrow…aren't you, Tony? I want a rematch on checkers and Chinese checkers!"

"You better practice with Holly if you're going to beat me," Tony teased.

"I guess he told you, Uncle Mel," Holly said with a laugh.

"I think I'll go to bed early tonight…so I'm well rested for our match off."

"Thanks again, Holly."

"Yes, thank you for making my day fun," Tony said smiling at Holly and Uncle Mel.

"It was our pleasure," Holly said.

CHAPTER 4

FRIDAY AFTERNOON

Holly had a very productive day of baking while Uncle Mel waited on Tony and she could hear them both laughing as they played Chinese checkers. She had never seen this side of Uncle Mel, and was loving every minute of it.

Before doing her baking that morning, she had made a large pan of Lasagna and decided she would invite Dan and his girls over for dinner again. He had accepted and offered to pick up some garlic bread to go with it.

With the lunch dishes completed, she had time to start on some shortbread and Danish butter cookies. She was keeping careful watch over the time so she wouldn't forget to put the Lasagna in the oven for dinner.

As she continued to work, even she had to admit the aromas in her kitchen were delightfully mouthwatering. She decided to fix a plate of some freshly baked cookies, along with a couple of bottled waters and placed them on a tray.

"Hello you two! Do you have time for a cookie break and some water?"

"Yes! Is that what I've been smelling all afternoon?" Tony asked.

"Holly makes the best cookies you'll ever eat!"

"Thank you, Uncle Mel. It's nice to cook and bake for people who appreciate it! How goes the Chinese checkers' battle?"

"Oh, we don't want to talk about that do we, Tony?"

"I don't have a problem talking about it, Uncle Mel! You might, though!"

"Pass the cookies," Mel said while winking at Tony.

"We're going to have Lasagna for dinner tonight. I was wondering, Tony, if you would like to try to come downstairs and eat with us? Your dad and sisters are coming for dinner too."

"Since I've been beating Uncle Mel at Chinese checkers, I'm feeling a lot better. I think I could make it down for dinner."

"Great! I'll set you a place at the table. You two have another hour and a half to play, and then it should be time for dinner."

"Sounds good," Tony and Uncle Mel echoed together.

Holly was enjoying her new job of being chief cook and bottle washer, plus hostess with the most-ess…and hoped when the inn officially opened that she would enjoy it as much or more. She had just finished setting the table when she heard a knock at the door.

"Hello Dan and the other T's! How's everybody doing tonight?"

"We're hungry and excited that we get to come over to your house again!" Tammy said happily.

"We could get used to this" Teri replied hopefully.

"We picked up a couple of loaves of garlic bread," Dan informed Holly. I had the bakery slice the bread, so we'll just need to toast it."

"Perfect! Come on in and I'll start getting the garlic bread toasted. Dan, will you go up and tell Uncle Mel and Tony we're ready to eat? Tony is feeling pretty good this afternoon and is going to try to come down and eat with us."

"Oh, that is great news. Come on girls, let's go get Tony."

Within five minutes everyone was gathered in the dining room ready for dinner. Holly was especially happy that Tony felt well enough to join them and was thrilled that Uncle Mel was enjoying being a part of the gathering.

As Holly listened to the girls share their experiences at school, she couldn't help wondering if this was what it was like to have your own family. She casually looked at Dan and could see the joy in his face as he listened to his children. Tony wasn't a bit shy and shared in detail about how he had beaten Uncle Mel in checkers and Chinese checkers. Uncle Mel was being such a good sport about it all!

When dinner was finished, Tony asked, "Holly, do we get to have some of your cookies for dessert?"

"I think that could be arranged."

"Wait 'til you taste her cookies...they are so fantastic!" Tony said while describing them in detail.

"I'm very impressed with your baking and cooking talents," Dan stated.

"For the last five years I cooked and baked for the Luxury Inn. So, you could say I've had a little bit of practice. I've been working at getting my baking for the Christmas holidays done." She had put aside some cookies, figuring she would serve them for dessert. She uncovered the plate and brought the cookies to the table. "These are shortbread and Danish butter cookies, enjoy!"

"Is there something we can help you do to get your inn ready for Christmas…and to pay back your kindness for helping us?" Dan asked.

"Tomorrow, Uncle Mel was going to begin putting up the Christmas lights…and I bet he'd love some help…isn't that right, Uncle Mel?"

"The more, the merrier!" Uncle Mel said happily.

"I'm sure we can lend a hand in whatever you need. How about we come over tomorrow around nine in the morning. Would that work?"

"Yes, that will be perfect!"

SATURDAY MORNING

Holly got up early in order to have some freshly baked cinnamon rolls ready for Dan and his children when they came over to help Uncle Mel put up the Christmas lights and garland.

Uncle Mel was dressed in his work clothes and she could tell he was happy by all the humming and whistling he was doing. Holly was wiping the kitchen counters when they heard knocking on the door.

"I'll get it," Uncle Mel called out. After opening the front door, she heard him say, "Now that's what I call a good-looking Christmas crew!"

"Mmmm...what smells so good?" Tammy asked, while walking inside and following her nose to the kitchen. "Did you make something special just for us, Holly?"

"I sure did! As soon as we get some Christmas lights and decorations up, we'll have some cinnamon rolls and hot chocolate or milk, whichever you prefer."

"I want milk!" Tammy said excitedly.

"I want hot chocolate!" Teri replied.

"Let's get started so we can have a treat as soon as possible," Uncle Mel said motioning for the kids to follow him.

"You can watch, Tony, but I don't want you doing any lifting...okay?" Dan warned him.

"I understand, Dad. I wish I could help."

"We're just happy to see you up and dressed, and you look like you're feeling a lot better. Are you, Tony?" Holly asked.

"Yes, I am. It's probably from all those yummy cookies I've been eating."

"I knew there had to be a good reason!" Holly said with a chuckle while looking at Dan.

43

"Do you want the girls to come with us, or here with you?" Dan asked.

"They can choose inside or outside. I'll be putting up some garland around the staircase and railing…along with making some Christmas wreaths."

"I want to help Holly," Tammy said jumping up and down.

"I'm going to see what the guys are doing, and then I'll probably be back," Teri advised.

"We'll be here," Holly said with a smile. "Follow me, Tammy, and we'll start putting up some pretty Christmas garland on the staircase." Tammy followed Holly to the den where the room was filled with all kinds of Christmas decorations.

"Wow…it looks like a Christmas store in this room," Tammy said in awe as she stared at everything.

"It sure does. Hopefully, we can get most of these Christmas decorations hung up today…so I can use this room again. Will you help me carry these garlands, Tammy?"

"Yes, I'm a good helper!"

"I can see that!"

A couple of hours soon flew by and Holly decided it was time for a cinnamon roll break. "Let's go outside and see how the guys are doing and tell them it's time for some cinnamon rolls…okay Tammy?"

"That's a great idea! I'll go tell them right now!"

Having children around at Christmas time sure made things exciting and extra fun! When Holly walked outside, she thought for sure she had stepped into a Christmas wonderland! When she looked at the roofline, her heart skipped a beat with joy to see the gorgeous green garlands draped perfectly with bright white lights wrapped around each garland proclaiming to all who would see it that the festive season had arrived again! There was something so special about the magic of Christmas!

As she turned to the entryway of the cabin, she admired the railings that led up to the front door which were also wrapped in the garland with white lights. All they needed now, were some perfectly tied red Christmas bows to set off each section.

"What do you think about what we've done so far?" Uncle Mel asked Holly.

"I love it! You have brought back the Christmas magic to our cabin! Tammy and I were wondering if you would like to come in for a cinnamon roll break?"

A chorus of "Yeses" could be heard loud and clear and they all rushed inside for a break.

"Wow…it looks like Christmas has appeared inside the cabin too," Dan and Uncle Mel said when they came in.

"Everyone wash your hands and be back here to get your cinnamon roll," Holly instructed.

It didn't take long until all were back at the table enjoying their treat. "I like helping you decorate, Holly," Teri said. "You feed us the best treats when we come over!"

"Uncle Mel and I can't thank you enough for all of your help. I'm sure it would have taken us a week to finish what you've been able to do in a couple of hours today."

"I'm the one who should be thanking them," Uncle Mel said. "Some of my bones and muscles don't work like they used to…and it takes me forever to get things done!"

"Are you going to get a Christmas tree?" Tammy asked.

"I've been thinking about it," Holly answered. "In fact, I called the city of Panguitch, and all I have to do is go over and get a permit, and I can go and cut down my own Christmas tree. I thought it would be neat to get a fresh Christmas tree this year…so the house would really smell like Christmas!"

"Would you cut it down all by yourself?" Teri asked in amazement.

"No…I probably would need some help."

"We could help you, couldn't we, Dad?" Teri and Tammy quickly volunteered.

"If Holly needs our help, I'm sure we could."

"I'm still thinking about it. It's expensive to go that route…and I'll need to review my finances before I make a final decision. It's also probably going to snow by the time I'm ready to get a tree…and I don't really want to deal with snow and a Christmas tree. There's a lot to think about!"

"I'm going to make a snowman as soon as we get enough snow," Tammy told everyone."

"Are you good at making snowmen?" Holly asked. "I may need you to make a cute snowman in front of the cabin in January. That would be a charming and welcoming decoration."

"I'll help her if you want me to," Teri volunteered.

"I sure am glad that your three T's ran into me that day we met at the warehouse, Dan! Look at all this good help I have now."

"You never told me how you met," Uncle Mel said.

"I think Tony could tell the story the best, don't you, Dan?"

"Yes, I think he definitely could!"

Soon they were all laughing when Tony told about the three tornados running into a very unsuspecting Holly as she was minding her own business.

"I think I'm very grateful the three T's ran into you, Holly. Our lives have changed for the better!"

"I agree with you Uncle Mel."

"I'd like to be able to beat one of the T's in a game of Chinese checkers...and one of these days, I will," Uncle Mel said with a big grin on his face.

Holly peeked at Tony and could tell he was delighted at Mel's comment.

"Well, we hate to eat and run, but we've got grocery shopping and laundry to do, plus some homework...so we should be on our way," Dan advised.

"Thanks so much for coming over. It's definitely beginning to look a lot like Christmas around here...as they say, and it's all thanks to you!"

"We were happy to help…and thanks for helping us last week."

"I hope to see you in church tomorrow."

"If we don't have any emergencies, we'll be there."

Uncle Mel and Holly stood at the front door and waved as Dan and his three T's climbed into their SUV and left.

"Uncle Mel, the garlands and lights look incredible. You and Dan did such a beautiful job of hanging them! I'm so pleased. How are you feeling about everything?"

"I feel great and I appreciate the compliment. I have to say, I am surprised at how much I've enjoyed getting to know Tony. He is quite a guy…and I think he helped me more than I helped him! I think Dan is a nice guy too and the other two T's are pretty special. What do you think of them, Holly?"

"I have to admit I wasn't happy the day they ran into me; but they do have a way of growing on you."

"Do you think you could fall for a guy like, Dan?"

"Uncle Mel, what are you talking about?"

"You know…falling in love, getting married?"

"Uncle Mel, that is the last thing on my mind right now. My main focus is getting the inn open and ready for business. Remember, I don't have a job right now…and we will run out of money if I'm not working."

"I just thought with Dan being a widower and such with three pretty nice kids, you might want to encourage the situation before he looks elsewhere."

"To be honest with you, Uncle Mel, I haven't even given it a second thought."

"Well, maybe you should."

"Right now, I've got to go to the printers and see if they have my flyers ready…so I can get them passed out to people/tourists who might be looking for a nice place to stay during the holidays and after. I also need to pick up my red Christmas bows from Ruby's so we can finish our decorations."

"Okay, Holly, but don't say I didn't tell you so, and blame me when he goes somewhere else because you were too busy opening your inn."

"I promise I won't, Uncle Mel, but right now I don't have time to think about that. I'm going to go and freshen up and then I'm going to run my errands."

CHAPTER 5

CHURCH/SUNDAY MORNING

Holly arrived at church an hour early on Sunday morning hoping to see the Bishop so she could ask him if it would be okay to pin one of her flyers to the weekly bulletin board, as well as, placing them next to the weekly announcements where anyone interested could pick one up.

She watched as the Bishop studied one of her flyers, and then looked at her and said, "Wow, Holly, that's quite an undertaking. Did you quit your job at the Luxury Inn?"

"Yes, I did. I have been saving for five years and planning carefully for the day I could turn my cabin into an inn. Of course, it won't be on the same level as the Luxury Inn, but I hope to provide a cozy home away from home atmosphere where my guests can enjoy homecooked meals and a personal touch of home."

"You have my permission to place your flyers out by the announcements, and I want to wish you much success Holly. I also understand from Arlene that you took in Tony Winthrop on Thursday and Friday. I wanted to thank you for your willingness to help, and ask how it went?"

"It turned out better than I could have imagined. My Uncle Mel has not been happy about my opening up the cabin as an inn, and he was angry when I told him Tony would be staying for a couple of days. The interesting part about this experience was, he and Tony got along very well together, and even started playing checkers and Chinese checkers. Dan and his children came over yesterday and helped us put up our Christmas lights, which was a huge help!"

"Miracles never cease do they? I know Dan has been quite concerned about how Tony would adjust to their move here, and it sounds like the time he spent with your Uncle Mel was just the right medicine."

"I have to agree with you there, Bishop. Thank you for allowing me to put my flyers out. Is it okay if I continue to do it off and on until my business gets going?"

"Yes, you can, Holly."

"I appreciate it so much, and I'll let you go as I'm sure you have lots to do before the service starts."

Holly took a seat close to the back of the sanctuary because she wanted to people watch and one of those people, she intended to watch was Dan Winthrop. Ever since her conversation with Uncle Mel yesterday, she couldn't stop thinking about Dan. Up to that point, she hadn't even considered a romance between them. If the truth were to be told, she had given up on finding love years ago.

Holly checked the time and saw that the service would be starting in about five minutes. She heard a little disturbance at the entrance to the sanctuary and three tornados had just touched down in the form of Tony, Teri, and Tammy. She smiled at their antics and couldn't help wondering where Dan was. About a minute later he came in with Kourtney Petersen at his side, and it was obvious that Kourtney's intent was to keep his undivided attention.

51

Kourtney looked every bit the model with her tall lean figure, and long beautifully styled blonde hair. She was dressed in a pink suit that hugged her perfect body and even wore pink shoes to match her outfit. Dan was looking around the congregation to see where his three T's had landed, and if it wasn't her imagination, he looked a little embarrassed and frustrated when he noticed she was watching him.

"We're over here Dad," Tammy yelled, and Holly giggled when she saw Dan put his finger to his mouth trying to remind her to talk softly. He moved quickly to take a seat on the row where his children were, and Holly found it even more interesting when he placed Tammy between himself and Kourtney on the bench. One thing was sure...even if the sermon was boring today, the view a few rows ahead of her certainly wouldn't be! The biggest question now, *why was she feeling jealous? Afterall, she had told Uncle Mel that she needed to focus on getting the inn ready for its opening, and the last thing she needed to be worried about was dating...and falling in love!*

When the sermon ended, Holly knew she wouldn't be able to tell anyone what it had been about, and hoped no one would ask. Her mind was so preoccupied with Dan Winthrop and his three T's...that she decided leaving early before the closing song and prayer would be a good idea.

On her way out, she glanced over at the reception area where the announcements were kept, and noticed with satisfaction that half of the flyers about the opening of her inn had been taken. On that thought, she would focus on the things that she could control and leave Dan Winthrop and his three T's to the likes of Kourtney Petersen.

52

SUNDAY EVENING

Holly was rocking away in her chair by the fireplace and thinking about the week ahead and all the things that still needed to be done before everything would be ready for the opening.

The phone interrupted her thoughts, and she got up to answer it.

"Hello Holly, this is Dan. I wanted to call and see how you're doing?"

"Hi Dan. I'm doing great! I was just sitting down by the fireplace making a list of all the things I need to do this upcoming week. How are you?"

"I'm doing good. I saw your flyer about the inn when I came into church. It's a great flyer...and I think it'll help bring you, business."

"I sure hope so! How's Tony feeling?"

"He's doing so much better...almost back to his old self. I have you and Uncle Mel to thank for that. He will still have to be careful for several weeks that he doesn't do anything too strenuous."

"Yes, I'm sure that's to be expected."

"I didn't see you after church...and was hoping to talk to you about a few things."

"I saw that you came in with Kourtney Petersen, and didn't want to be a third wheel...if you know what I mean."

"About that…I hope you'll believe me when I tell you that that was all her idea…not mine. I was worried that you would get the wrong impression…and wanted to call and set things right."

"You don't have to do that, Dan. It's not like we're going steady or engaged…you know."

"Would you like to be?"

"I'm not sure how to answer that question, Dan. Would you like to be?"

"I know it's very early in our relationship…but if the truth were told, the answer would be YES! From the first moment we ran into you…and you know that I mean that literally, you've been on my mind constantly. I love how you treat my children, you're gorgeous, you can cook like nobody else, you're kind and generous…and I'm falling in love with you! Do you by chance have any feelings for me and my three tornados?"

"When I first met you, I thought about how handsome you were…and still are. I enjoy being around your tornados…and have learned to love their antics. I have to admit when I saw you walk into church with Kourtney Petersen today, I was jealous. It surprised me that I had those feelings because I had given up on finding love many years ago."

"You don't know how much better that makes me feel. I was sick to my stomach when Kourtney was hanging all over me…and then I looked for my kids and saw you looking at me. I hope you saw that I placed Tammy between us…so you'd get the idea that Kourtney and I are not a thing."

"I think you'll need to let Kourtney know that."

"I did...and I'm sure her feelings have completely changed about me by now. Enough about her...it's you, dear Holly, that I want to focus on. I didn't mean for all of this to spill out over the phone, but I've been worried all day about it. I have feelings for you, and I want to court you and take all the time we need to cultivate our feelings for each other. I want to be a part of your dreams...and I want you to be a part of mine. I'm an accountant and I could help you set up your business if that's something you'd like."

"That's so incredible, Dan, that you should mention that. I've been dreading that part of the business...and even had a few nightmares about it! I've actually been praying for help to know where I should go for help! You're an answer to my prayers, Dan."

"Well, you are definitely an answer to my prayers, Holly! I know we're moving fast...and I want to take things at a pace that is comfortable for you. I was concerned that you would get the wrong impression today when you saw me with Kourtney. She is not the girl for me...it's you, Holly, that I want in my life. I needed to call and set the record straight. Can we say for now that we're going steady?"

"Yes, I like that, Dan."

"Good. That way, we can move at our own pace, continue to get to know each other, and if we both still like each other, we'll get more serious."

"That works for me. I'm so glad you called, Dan."

"I have one more question for you. Thanksgiving is just around the corner, if I buy a turkey, will you cook it...and can I and my three T's spend Thanksgiving with you?"

"I would love that, and I know Uncle Mel will love it. I would also like the kids to spend Wednesday, the day before Thanksgiving, here with me…so we can spend the day cooking, playing, and getting ready for Thanksgiving. Do you think they'd like that?"

"I'm sure they'd love it! I'm so happy that I called you and you shared that you do have feelings for me. I'll let you get back to making your to do lists…and will you please include me on those lists so I can help you with your inn? I want to be a part of everything you do so you can enjoy your inn…and me, and our three T's."

CHAPTER 6

THANKSGIVING WEEK

Holly was cleaning up the breakfast dishes when she found herself humming and whistling! It reminded her of Uncle Mel a few weeks ago when she heard him whistling and humming! It felt wonderful to have something to be happy about…enough to make you want to hum and whistle!

For the past two weeks, Dan and his three T's had come over every night for dinner…and each night she had a list of "honey do's" that needed to be done. It was thrilling to see Uncle Mel, Dan, and Tony work together as a team to take care of each item on her list.

Holly had set up several long tables in her den area where she had placed wreaths that needed little ornaments, sprigs of berries, and a Christmas bow added to them with hot glue to complete them. Teri and Tammy dug into the boxes that contained these items and carefully set them by each wreath so all Holly had to do was use her glue gun and attach them.

"You girls are the best helpers I could ever ask for! Thank you so much for helping me get these wreaths looking so pretty!"

"We like helping you, Holly! You make it fun!" Tammy exclaimed.

"We're kind of like your Christmas elves, Holly," Teri replied happily.

"You certainly are…and just like Christmas elves, you deserve a special treat when we're finished!"

"Really, Holly? I wonder what it will be?" the girls whispered curiously to each other.

When the last wreath got its Christmas bow, ornaments, and a sprig of berries, Holly announced it was time to go and wash up and head for the kitchen.

"I made some glazed doughnuts today and some apple cider. There's also milk or hot chocolate if you'd rather have that. How does that sound?"

"I can't wait! Can I go tell daddy and Tony what we get to have?" Tammy asked excitedly?

"Can I go with her?" Teri asked eagerly.

"You can both go…and then come back and help me!"

"We will!" they shouted as they ran to find the boys.

A few minutes later, Dan, Uncle Mel, and Tony came into the kitchen…wanting to know, "Hey what's all this talk about doughnuts and apple cider?"

"Don't forget milk and hot chocolate," Teri quickly added.

"I have to pay my workers with some yummy treats…or you might not come back to help me tomorrow…right?"

"You mean we have that option?" Dan asked kiddingly.

"No, that option is not available!" Holly said with a big chuckle! Go wash your hands, while the girls and I get everything ready."

Holly was finding more and more to love about her helpers each day, and wondered how she ever managed without them.

Dan had surprised her the previous weekend, and arranged a night out on the town while Tony and Uncle Mel babysat the girls. It had been so long since Holly had gone out on a date to dinner, that she felt nervous and was sure she was acting just like a teenager on a first date. Thankfully Dan didn't seem to notice and treated her like a queen.

They decided they would go to Bull's Restaurant for dinner and each ordered a rib steak with a baked potato and a small salad. It felt strange and somewhat lonely without the three T's and Uncle Mel to keep things lively and entertaining. "I guess I never noticed how quiet it is without Uncle Mel and the three T's," Holly commented while they were eating their salad.

"I was noticing that too. I am enjoying your company and not constantly being interrupted," Dan said looking into her lovely face.

Speaking of interruptions, the waiter brought over their steaks and they hurried to move their salads so he could put the hot plates on the table.

"Are you glad you made the move to Panguitch, Utah, Dan?"

"I am now, especially since I met you, Holly. I was a little worried at first that the change might have been too drastic for Tony. When I look back on the past couple of months, it's been a blessing…even with Tony having to have surgery. I would have never gotten to know you this quickly, and with Tony having to be dependent on someone other than me and his sisters, it forced him to come out of his shell."

"Even Uncle Mel admitted that he thought Tony had done more for him than he did for Tony."

"I would probably debate him on that. I've never seen Tony take to someone as quickly as he did Uncle Mel."

"I think it's because they are both hermits!"

Dan chuckled at her comment. "Yes…and hermits know exactly when to talk and when to be quiet."

"How's your dinner?" Holly asked.

"I can tell you truthfully, I would rather eat your cooking any day of the week…than this! You may want to reconsider opening an inn…and just do cooking for some of these restaurants in Panguitch. Have you ever thought about that?"

"Yes and no. I've always had compliments on my cooking, but I didn't want to have to drive around and deliver my goods to all the restaurants. I like the idea of keeping it all in one place where I can cook and serve and not have to leave home."

"I can understand that. Once the inn opens, you'll have to see how it all goes, and if it doesn't work out the way you hoped, there's always an option of selling your baked goods to the local restaurants."

"I agree, Dan, it's always good to have more than one option."

"Tell me more about yourself, Holly. Do you have any siblings?"

"No, I'm an only child. I always wished I had a brother or sister. How about you, Dan?"

"I have a brother and sister and both are older than me. They live in Colorado with their families."

"What did you do for fun while growing up?"

"I loved to play baseball and my dad had a boat and we would take it out and go fishing quite often."

"What did you do while growing up, Holly?"

"My mom loved to cook and sew…and I learned how to knit and crochet from her. My dad liked to see beautiful country so we were always taking little vacations to Bryce, Zion, and Grand Canyon. Cedar Breaks isn't too far from Panguitch and is also gorgeous. Have you ever been there, Dan?"

"No, but it sounds like I need to."

After dinner, they decided to take a walk and Dan reached for her hand. "Since we're going steady, I thought it would be okay to hold your hand."

Holly looked up into Dan's face and said, "I'd love to hold your hand." His hand was warm and firm and it felt secure and reassuring to walk with someone she had grown to admire.

"I have really enjoyed coming over with my three terrors every night, eating dinner with you and Uncle Mel, and then working together on your inn to get it ready. I know the kids have enjoyed it as well."

"I can't wait to see you each night and the three T's too. I'm happy you asked me to go steady with you, Dan."

"How happy, Holly?"

She paused to look up at him, and he surprised her by pulling her close and bringing his lips to hers. It started off as a wonderful kiss and turned passionate. "I love you, dear Holly. I'm so happy the Lord pushed our paths together. You'll never know the joy you have brought into my life and the three T's. Thank you, Holly." He lowered his head and captured her lips again.

"I love you too, Dan, and your little tornados. I don't know how, but all of you have captured a piece of my heart. Thank you for being you…and for loving me! I'm excited to see where our relationship takes us!"

Holly loved thinking about her special moments with Dan while she finished doing the dishes. When everything was put away, she decided she better get out her Thanksgiving recipes and start making a grocery list of all the items she would need to pick up so she'd be ready for the three T's on Wednesday when they came over to help her cook.

WEDNESDAY AFTERNOON

"I never knew Thanksgiving was so much work," Teri said to Holly. "I just thought it was a holiday where you eat a lot of food!"

"I didn't like Thanksgiving when I was growing up," Holly told the girls.

"Why not?"

"I thought it was a holiday where you had to wash every pot and pan, and every dish in the house. One Thanksgiving I ate so much, I thought I would never feel good again!"

She loved hearing the girls' laughter. "You're funny, Holly. We love hearing about when you were little."

"I'm glad you two are having fun. Okay, let's check to see what we've done. So far, we made the cranberry salad, and the sweet potatoes, now it's time to make the stuffing that's going to go inside the turkey. Once we finish that, I made some pizzas that we can put in the oven for our dinner tonight. Your daddy should be getting home from work any time now."

"He's going to be so surprised to see how much we've done. He loves pumpkin pie. Are we going to make any of those?"

"Oh Teri, I'm so glad you reminded me. We can make those next and they can bake while we're eating pizza."

Soon they were pouring the pumpkin pie batter into the crust filled pie pans, when they heard a knock on the front door. "I bet that's daddy," the girls said together. "Can we go to the door and let him in?"

"You sure can."

Holly loved hearing them greet Dan and listening to their excited chatter as they shared the events of their day with him.

"Hello Dan!"

"How's my favorite cook?" Dan said with a smile on his face. "Are we having pizza for Thanksgiving?"

"No silly! We're having pizza for tonight's dinner…and the rest of the stuff is for our Thanksgiving dinner tomorrow."

"Oh good…I was worried for a minute. Speaking of Thanksgiving, I need to bring in the turkey."

"Is it frozen?"

"Yes."

"We need to get it into the bathtub where I have a large tote, so it can start thawing out for tomorrow. Go and get it, and I'll get the water running in the tote."

"I didn't know the turkey had to take a bath before you cook it," Teri said.

Tammy held the door open for Dan and soon Holly had an audience as they watched Dan place the turkey in the large tote in the bathtub. "Okay, Mr. Turkey, take a bath so we can have you for Thanksgiving tomorrow!"

"That's the funniest thing I ever saw!" Teri said.

"Tomorrow, I hope it's one of the most delicious things you ever saw and ate for Thanksgiving," Holly said while winking at her.

Their evening was filled with lots of fun and family laughter as they ate dinner and talked about previous Thanksgivings. The pumpkin pies were cooling on racks after being baked to perfection. "I think we've finished all of our holiday cooking jobs and now we're ready and prepared for Thanksgiving day," Holly announced happily.

"Do we have time to play a game, Holly?" Tammy asked.

"Hmmm...let me think of a game that we can all play," Holly said.

"Let's do a game you used to do when you were a little girl," Teri replied.

"I know a game I think you'll love. It was one of my favorites when I was growing up. I'll be right back."

Everyone watched curiously as Holly left the room and wondered what game it would be.

Holly came back with a big smile on her face and said, "Okay everyone, gather around and look what's in my hand. Does anyone know what it is?"

The three T's shook their heads no, and Holly said, "It's a thimble that my mother and grandmother used when they did their sewing. Unless you do a lot of sewing, most people don't know what they are anymore."

"Are we going to sew?" Teri asked looking confused.

"No, we're going to play, "hide the thimble". Now when it's your turn to hide the thimble, you need to hide it in a spot that can be plainly seen. That means, you don't have to touch or move anything to find it. If no one sees it after about five minutes, then hot and cold clues can be used to help you find it. I'll be the first to hide it so you can see how it's going to work. Everyone follow Uncle Mel to the family room and I'll hide the thimble in plain sight in the living room. I'll call you once I have hidden it."

As she listened to their excitement, it brought back happy memories of when she played the game as a little girl with her parents and cousins. "Okay, you can come back to the living room and look for it."

Tammy and Teri raced back to the living room and immediately started looking. "Remember you don't have to move anything. If you do see the thimble, don't tell anyone, just take a seat on the couch or a chair until everyone else finds it."

The room was very quiet as everyone concentrated on looking for the thimble. "This game is hard," Tammy said.

"Okay, I'm going to give you some hot and cold clues. If I tell you someone is hot…that means that where they are looking, they are getting closer to finding the thimble. If I tell you someone is getting cold, that means they're looking in the wrong area for the thimble. Right now Tony is getting warmer."

Everyone quickly rushed over to where Tony was looking. Tony kept looking, and Holly knew the second he saw it. "Remember, if you see it, go sit down…and when the game is over, you'll get to go and get it."

Within seconds, Tony took a seat on the couch. "How did you do that so fast, Tony?" Teri asked.

"Now Uncle Mel is the warmest." Uncle Mel turned quickly around and went and sat by Tony on the couch. "Tammy's getting warmer."

"I am?" Tammy asked shocked.

Teri got next to Tammy and kept looking until she saw it. By now Dan was over by Tammy and pointed Tammy's head in the right spot until she saw it. "That was a good spot!" Tammy said with a chuckle.

"Okay everyone, let Tony go get it…so he can prove he really found it."

Tony got up confidently and walked over and proudly showed everyone the thimble. "Good job, Tony, now it's your turn to hide it. What do you need to remember?"

"Hide it in plain sight."

"You got it! Come on everyone, let's go back to the den. Tony will call us when it's hidden."

They played several more games until everyone had an opportunity to hide the thimble. After the last game Dan announced, "Okay, it's time for us to go home so Holly and Uncle Mel can get some rest. Tomorrow's a big day with it being Thanksgiving."

"I hope we can play "hide the thimble" some more tomorrow," Tammy said hopefully.

"I'm sure we'll be able to. I want to thank my cooks today for helping me get our Thanksgiving feast ready for tomorrow. Let's plan on eating between three and four tomorrow, afternoon. You can come over any time after two o'clock."

"We'll be here. You kids run out to the car while I talk to Holly for a few minutes. Goodnight, Uncle Mel."

When Uncle Mel had left the room, Dan couldn't wait to wrap Holly in his arms. "Thank you for making our Thanksgiving season so much fun! My three T's will have the best memories from all the time they got to spend with you today. From giving the turkey a bath to baking pumpkin pies...you are the best, Miss Holly." He lowered his lips to hers and kissed and hugged the puddin' out of her. "I love you, Holly, and I thank my lucky stars every day that I found you!"

"I love you too, Dan, and it's so much fun to have a family to do all these fun things with. Thank you!" They hugged and kissed again, pulling apart when they heard a constant car horn. "It sounds like the three tornados are getting restless!" Holly giggled.

"It sure does. I'll see you tomorrow, Holly."

"Goodnight, Dan."

CHAPTER 7

THANKSGIVING DAY

Holly woke up happy and thankful on Thanksgiving morning. Never in her wildest dreams, would she have imagined all the wonderful blessings that were coming her way.

She slipped out of bed so she could kneel and say a prayer of thanks for her parents who had left her this beautiful cabin, for the miracle that had come over Uncle Mel and the joy and happiness she had seen in him recently, and for the gift of Dan and his three T's. In another week her inn would be open to the public and she wondered if she would have any guests. So far no one had called to make a reservation. She knew she only had the four rooms…and wondered if she should consider cooking and baking for the local restaurants rather than having people stay at the inn. If she did marry Dan, she didn't want to miss out on the family time she had experienced this week with the kids. This would be her only opportunity to be a mother…and she was loving every minute of it. If they married, where would they live? He was renting a small home right now. There were still so many things to think about and a lot of decisions to be made. However, today was a holiday, Thanksgiving, and she didn't have to make any big decisions right now. Today was a day to be enjoyed, to express thanks for all the blessings and miracles she had in her life!

Holly was in the kitchen, dressed and ready to make breakfast after having showered. She remembered the turkey was still in the bathtub in a tote and decided to go and check to see if it was thawed out yet. She could still feel some slightly frozen areas and was glad their dinnertime wasn't until three in the afternoon. The turkey would need another couple of hours thawing time, and three to four hours of cooking. Everything was right on schedule.

When she walked back into the kitchen, Uncle Mel was sitting at the table. "Good morning, Uncle Mel. Happy Thanksgiving. How are you doing today?"

"I'm doing great. How are you, Holly?"

"I'm happy and looking forward to our Thanksgiving feast. Have you enjoyed having Dan and his family here?"

"I have really grown fond of those kids, and Dan too. I hope you don't mind my asking; are you and Dan getting serious?"

"We're going steady."

"What does that mean, Holly?"

"It means we want to date each other exclusively…to see if we really do want to marry and share our lives together."

"And how do you feel about it so far?"

"Every day I'm finding that I'm more and more in love with Dan and the three T's. This is probably my only opportunity to be a mother…and I'm loving every second of it. I realize we're in the early fun stage of it all, and it's not always going to be fun and games. How are you enjoying it, Uncle Mel?"

"I'm surprised at how much I'm enjoying it too! If you had asked me a year ago if I would have liked or wanted this situation, I would have said no way!"

"I guess we're both learning that when we forget ourselves, and serve others, or in our case, serve these children, we are truly finding ourselves and the joy that comes with it! I just don't know how it's all going to work out with trying to run an inn, and be a mother at the same time. I'm a little bit scared, Uncle Mel."

"Have you talked to Dan about your feelings?"

"Yes, and no. The other night when you babysat and we went out to dinner together, he asked me if I had ever considered making baked goods or cooking for the local restaurants. He told me I cook way better than any restaurant he's been to so far. In some ways I'm leaning in that direction now...so I can be a mother and enjoy these kids. There's so much to think and pray about. For today, I'm just going to enjoy this wonderful Thanksgiving day. I will pray about what I should do...and I know I will be guided in the right direction."

"I'll say one thing for you, Holly, you've always had a good head on your shoulders. I want you to know that I will help you in any way I can."

"That means a lot to me, Uncle Mel. I love you...and I'm thankful for you."

"Right back at you, Holly."

THANKSGIVING DINNER

71

The turkey was in the oven baking, the potatoes had been peeled and were on the stove cooking, the dining room table had been set, and the cabin was filled with the delightful aromas of Thanksgiving. There was a knock on the door, and Uncle Mel shouted, "I'll get it, Holly."

Holly turned in time to see Uncle Mel race to the door and couldn't help the giggle that erupted from inside her as she witnessed his excitement to welcome Dan and his three T's.

"Happy Thanksgiving Uncle Mel! Wow it, sure smells like Thanksgiving in this house!" Tammy and Teri shouted. "Where's Holly?"

"She's in the kitchen," Uncle Mel replied. "How's Tony and Dan on this Thanksgiving day?"

"We're hungry," Dan replied happily.

"I could eat the whole turkey by myself," Tony said to Uncle Mel.

"Is that right? Maybe I'll grab the mashed potatoes and gravy and we can go play Chinese checkers and eat turkey and potatoes while I beat you!" Uncle Mel chuckled.

"You better grab a pumpkin pie too, if you're going to beat me!" Tony responded with a huge laugh.

"Come on in…and welcome! Happy Thanksgiving," Uncle Mel replied happily.

They joined Holly in the kitchen anxious to be a part of the Thanksgiving activity. "I think the turkey is done. Would you like to pull it out of the oven, Dan?"

"I'd love to."

"Let me get you some hot pads, and you can set it over on this counter and we'll let it cool for a few minutes."

Dan had quite an audience as he carefully placed the turkey on the counter.

"How come its in a plastic bag?" Teri asked.

"I like to bake it that way so all the juices stay in one place and I can make lots of gravy."

"This is the funniest turkey I've ever seen. First it had a bath…and now it's cooking in a bag," Teri said shaking her head in amusement.

"The bag also keeps the turkey very moist so it practically melts in your mouth when you eat it." Holly started to cut the bag open, and was soon able to pour the liquid into a large pan that she placed on the stove to begin heating so she could make mouthwatering gravy.

It wasn't long before everything was ready and everyone was seated at the table for the Thanksgiving feast. After the prayer was said and the food passed around the table, Dan said, "I would like to start a tradition of each of us taking a turn to tell what we're thankful for. Does anyone want to start?"

"I do, I do," Tammy said excitedly raising her hand.

"Okay, sweetheart, why don't you start us off."

"I'm thankful and glad it's Thanksgiving…so we could learn how to cook this dinner with Holly…and I especially am thankful that she taught us how to play "hide the thimble".

"Can I go next?" Teri asked.

"Yes."

"I'm thankful for the new friends I've made at school. I was worried that no one would like me when we moved here. I really like spending time with Holly. She makes everything fun and I love to eat everything she makes! I wouldn't mind if she was part of our family...and you too, Uncle Mel."

Holly smiled and thought she might cry.

Dan looked at Tony, and Tony cleared his voice. "I'm thankful that I crashed into you, Holly, that day we met...or we might be eating tuna fish today!" Everyone at the table couldn't help but laugh. "I know I don't say a whole lot...but I'm really thankful that you volunteered to let me come and stay when I was recovering from my surgery. I felt welcome in your home and you acted like you really cared about me...and it made me feel good...even better. I really like you Uncle Mel...and would love it if we could become a family."

Uncle Mel cleared his throat and said, "I would like to go next...if that's alright. I've been grumpy and ornery for as long as I can remember, and Holly has put up with me all these years. I wasn't happy about her idea of turning this cabin into an inn, but if she hadn't, I never would have met Dan and the three T's. I can honestly say, that I love the whole lot of you! Holly has even commented on my humming and whistling...because since you've come into our lives, I'm happy! I'll be forever grateful for that. Oh and one more thing, I found me a wonderful boy, who loves to play checkers and Chinese checkers with me...and it makes me happy."

Dan looked at Holly, and saw the tears rolling down her cheeks. He reached into a pants pocket and took out a clean handkerchief and handed it to her. "I think it's your turn, Holly."

"My heart is so full and so thankful…for each one of you at this table. I woke up so happy this morning, and had to slip out of bed and thank the Lord for the day you crashed into me. I love each one of you so much, and can't believe all the joy you have brought into Uncle Mel's and my life. We love being a family with you and sharing this Thanksgiving day. I hope it will be the first of many more special holidays together!"

Everyone looked at Dan, and he said, "I guess that means it's my turn. This is a very special Thanksgiving…one that I think we will remember for many years to come. It has been a challenging year for all of us, but now it's turning into a wonderful year for our family. When I made the decision to move to Panguitch, Utah, I really had no idea why. I just felt an impression that this is where the Lord wanted our family. I was so worried that day when we ran into poor Holly that we were going to be kicked out of this state. Little did I know what a blessing it was that we did run into you. Holly, words cannot say enough about how kind and special you have been to each of us. I googled the word holly and found the following definition. Holly leaves and berries reflect the light and add color to the dark days of Yule. This is one reason people bring it into their homes. The berries became associated with the drops of blood shed for humanity's salvation. This is related in the Christmas carol, 'The Holly and the Ivy'. I think it's appropriate to what Holly has done for our family. She has brought the light and color back into our lives."

Dan pushed his chair back, and then knelt down beside Holly. "Holly, it's obvious that everyone here at this table wants to be a family. I wasn't sure when I was going to do this, but I can't think of a better time than now." He reached into another pants pocket and removed a small velvet box. He opened it slowly, and turned it toward Holly and asked, "Holly, I love you and would like you to be my wife. Will you marry me?"

"Oh Dan, I would love to be your wife so I can have you and the three T's around me forever!"

"I was hoping you would say that!"

Everyone at the table cheered…and Dan slipped the gorgeous diamond ring on Holly's finger. Holly stared at it, and couldn't believe it had a beautiful round center diamond, with a small red ruby on each side.

Dan noticed her staring at the ring and said, "The rubies represent holly berries…and you, precious Holly. He leaned down and gave Holly a tender kiss.

"I'm ready for some pumpkin pie!" Tony said.

"I'll munch to that," Uncle Mel replied with a chuckle.

"Who wants to help me whip the cream?" Holly asked.

Tammy and Teri hurried to her side and soon the whipping cream was whipped and she had two darling girls each licking a beater.

The rest of the day floated by in a blur of happiness for Holly. Somehow the food got put away and the dishes washed. She and Dan went for a walk while the three T's and Uncle Mel played "hide the thimble".

Once Dan and Holly were a short distance away, they hurried into each other's arms. They exchanged kisses and hugs and loving words to each other. "I'm so glad we have some time alone," Dan said. "There's so many things I want to say and talk about. How are you feeling about everything, Holly?"

"I'm happy, excited, and scared."

"What are you afraid of?" Dan asked with concern.

"I want to be a good mother...and I'm not sure how I'm going to juggle everything with trying to run an inn too."

"I've been thinking a lot about that myself. Can I share my thoughts with you?"

"Yes, please do."

"Is your heart set on opening an inn, Holly?"

"It was before I met you, and began loving the three T's. Now I'm thinking more about your idea of just making and selling baked goods for some of the local restaurants. I've been worried too about where we're all going to live."

"I make good money, Holly, and you don't have to work unless you want to. I sold my home in Colorado, and have all the proceeds from that in a sizeable money market account making excellent interest. I decided to rent when I moved here to make sure I would like it and the three T's would adapt to all the changes. So far, I think we all love it and want to stay here. How would you feel about letting each of the kids have a room upstairs in the cabin along with Uncle Mel, and you and I could remodel your downstairs bedroom and Uncle Mel's room into a large master bedroom and bath for us? I was also wondering how big your lot is?"

"The cabin sits on three acres...so there's plenty of room to expand."

"Would you like it if we contracted a builder to build you your own industrial kitchen close to the cabin where you could do all your baking and cooking for other restaurants if you decide you want to do that?"

"I'm loving all of your ideas, Dan. Are you sure about all of this?"

"I'm sure I want to help you make your dreams come true, and you're helping to make my dreams come true. When can I marry you, Holly? I'm ready right now...you just name the day."

"It would be nice to be married before Christmas. Why don't we get married in two weeks? I think for now I'll postpone the opening of the inn. Let's give ourselves time to get settled and readjusted to our new life together. We can take a look at our finances and see what we really want or need to do. I've always wanted to be a mother, and if I have a choice, I want to focus all of my time, love, and energy into being the best wife and mother I can."

"You certainly won't hear any complaints from me, dear Holly." Dan pulled Holly into his arms and they sealed their plans with more kisses and hugs!

CHAPTER 8

THE FIRST WEEK OF DECEMBER

The word spread quickly about Dan and Holly's engagement. They were fortunate to be able to meet with the Bishop before church started on Sunday and he was thrilled to learn of their upcoming marriage. He also agreed to perform the ceremony which would be held at the cabin for a small gathering of friends and family the following Saturday afternoon.

Holly removed the flyer from the bulletin board and picked up the extra flyers that were next to the Sunday announcements. So far, she hadn't received any phone calls about booking a reservation to stay at the inn and she wondered if the inn would have been able to provide a steady income for her and Uncle Mel after all.

Dan left her at the church while he went and picked up the three T's. The service was just about ready to start when she heard a slight disturbance at the side door and realized that her soon to be tornados had arrived! Dan rolled his eyes at their antics and Holly winked her love and approval when their eyes met.

When church was over, they went back to the cabin to eat lunch. Holly had made a turkey dressing casserole ahead of time and placed it in the oven to bake. While it was baking, Holly changed her clothes, and Dan had brought a change of clothes for the children and himself.

Everyone helped set the table for lunch, even Uncle Mel, wanting to be a part of this new family. Dan offered the blessing on the food and Uncle Mel asked, "Were you two able to meet with the Bishop before church?"

"Yes. He was very happy and excited to hear about our upcoming wedding and has agreed to perform the ceremony," Holly informed him.

"When is that going to happen?" Uncle Mel asked.

"We're going to be married here at the cabin this coming Saturday at two in the afternoon. It's going to be a small gathering of just family and a few friends from church."

"Where are we going to live after you marry Holly, Daddy?"

"Holly and I decided we would like to have everyone live here at the cabin."

Holly immediately noticed Uncle Mel lift his eyes, wondering how all that was going to work...along with the opening of the cabin.

"How's that going to work with opening the cabin for business?" Mel asked curiously.

"For right now, Dan and I have decided to postpone turning the cabin into an inn. We've decided to let each of the kids and Uncle Mel have their own room upstairs. Dan and I plan to do some remodeling downstairs where we will enlarge my bedroom and convert Uncle Mel's bedroom into an adjoining bathroom to the master bedroom."

"Wow...that sounds exciting," Teri and Tammy said with eyes big as saucers.

"I've decided for right now...I want to be a wife and mother first...and if I want to later on, we will build an industrial kitchen onto some of the extra land close to the cabin where I can do some cooking and baking to sell to various restaurants in Panguitch."

"Will you take us to school and go to back-to-school nights?" Teri asked.

"Would you like that?" Holly asked.

"I would love that! I want to have a mommy like all the other kids."

"I want to be there for all of your activities." She looked up and noticed that Tony had a sad look on his face. "I think it's important that we never forget your mommy who passed away, and I will try to take good care of you like she would want you to be taken care of." Tony's expression lightened up and she could tell that he had been worried about never forgetting his mother...and it was important to her also to always keep her memory alive.

"Do we have to take down the Christmas decorations and put up, wedding decorations?" Teri asked.

"I think the Christmas decorations will be beautiful for our wedding day. What do you think?"

"I'm glad to hear that," Teri said with a sigh. "That would have been a lot of work to have to redo everything!"

Everyone laughed! "We certainly don't want to have to do more work than we have to," Dan said with a chuckle.

After lunch, everyone went upstairs to look at all the bedrooms. "I would really like to have the bedroom I stayed in while I was getting better from my surgery," Tony said.

"Consider it done," Holly said.

"I would like to take the bedroom next to my buddy, Tony," Uncle Mel quickly added."

"I think that can be arranged," Holly agreed.

"Let's go look at the last two bedrooms," Dan said while taking Teri's and Tammy's hands. "Wow, I think you two got the best bedrooms of all!"

Both girls looked pleased and Holly was relieved that everything was going well. There was only one bathroom upstairs and Holly said, "The boys can use this bathroom, and the girls can share the downstairs bathroom with Dan and I until we get our new bathroom built."

"What if I have to go to the bathroom in the middle of the night?" Tammy asked with a worried look on her face.

"Go ahead and use the bathroom upstairs."

"We'll use this week to start moving our things over. Would you be willing to watch all of the T's while we go on a short honeymoon, Uncle Mel?" Dan asked.

"I'll be happy to watch them…and they can watch me too!" The three T's all laughed over his comment.

"We'll take good care of you, Uncle Mel," Teri said.

HOLLY & DAN'S WEDDING DAY

It was a gorgeous December day for a wedding. Mother nature had left a dusting of snow overnight, and the trees were covered in little ice crystals which added to their festive holiday décor.

Holly was bustling around the cabin making sure everything was ready. She couldn't believe she was really going to be married by the end of the day, and would become a mother to three beautiful children. She had grown to love each child with their unique personality and wonderful qualities. She hoped they would love her too.

She couldn't get over how helpful and supportive Uncle Mel had become. At times she wondered if he had turned into a completely different person. It was a good reminder of how love and feeling needed could change a person for the better.

"Hello Holly…or should I say the soon to be Mrs. Winthrop?"

"Hello Uncle Mel. I still can't believe all the wonderful changes that have happened to us…can you?"

"It's a miracle…is the only way I know how to describe it."

"Uncle Mel, are you happy?"

"Yes, dear Holly, I never dreamed I could be this happy. I love the three T's as if they were my own."

"It makes me so happy to hear you say that."

"You better go and get ready, Holly. I don't want to walk you down the aisle in your pajamas!"

"You're right! Dan might grab the three T's and run the other way!"

Holly was putting the last finishing touches to her hair. She wore a cream-colored suit and added a Christmas plaid necklace and earrings to spruce up her Christmas wedding attire. She slipped her feet into red pumps to finish her look and was pleased with what she saw in the mirror.

There was a knock on the door, and Uncle Mel asked if he could come in.

"You look beautiful, Holly. I don't think I've ever seen you look this stunning. I think marriage is going to look good on you!"

"Thank you, Uncle Mel. You cleaned up very nicely yourself."

"Whenever you're ready, my dear, your groom, soon to be children, and guests are all waiting for you to make your appearance."

"I'm ready, Uncle Mel, Holly said as she slipped her arm through his.

There was a hushed silence when Uncle Mel and Holly came into the living room. Everyone looked happy and ready for a wedding, and Holly couldn't have been happier. When she approached Dan, he handed her a gorgeous bouquet of red poinsettias that set off her cream suit and Christmas plaid jewelry.

The Bishop performed a touching ceremony and ended it by pronouncing them man and wife. Soon Dan pulled her close and sealed their "I do's" with a marital kiss and everyone clapped and cheered with joy.

After receiving congratulations, Tammy quickly reminded them that they needed to cut their wedding cake. It was a beautiful white cake with raspberry filling and the outside was decorated in white buttercream frosting with stunning red poinsettias added for the Christmas holiday time.

Soon it was time for Dan and Holly to leave and Uncle Mel reassured them that all would be well...and to enjoy their alone time.

EPILOGUE

Holly and Dan had the most wonderful wedding and honeymoon that year. Christmas came soon after and they began their holidays together by getting a permit and going up into the local mountains to cut down a fresh Christmas pine tree.

Their home smelled like Christmas and Christmas love could be felt within. There were many Christmas programs that Dan and Holly attended enjoying the three T's in their performances.

Many a night, laughter could be heard throughout the house as Uncle Mel and Tony challenged each other to Chinese checkers! The girls had received a large Barbie doll house for Christmas that year and were loving each minute they spent playing with it.

Dan and Holly were happy and enjoying their new life together. When the new year started, contractors would begin the renovations on their new master bedroom and attached bathroom.

Holly was staying very busy in her new role as wife and mother...and so far, had decided that it was enough for her as she loved and was enjoying being a part of her children's lives.

She loved her cabin and it had turned into the Christmas Inn she had always wanted...where there was always room for love!

Made in the USA
Monee, IL
10 August 2024

63650828R00059